William Leighton

Kormak, - An Icelandic Romance of the Tenth Century

in Six Cantos

William Leighton

Kormak, - An Icelandic Romance of the Tenth Century
in Six Cantos

ISBN/EAN: 9783337051686

Printed in Europe, USA, Canada, Australia, Japan

Cover: Foto ©Andreas Hilbeck / pixelio.de

More available books at **www.hansebooks.com**

KORMAK,

AN ICELANDIC ROMANCE

OF THE

TENTH CENTURY.

IN SIX CANTOS.

BOSTON:
WALKER, WISE, AND COMPANY,
245 WASHINGTON STREET.
1861.

University Press, Cambridge :
Stereotyped and Printed by Welch, Bigelow, & Co.

PREFACE.

DURING the eighth, ninth, and tenth
centuries, and later, the Scandinavians —
rude, barbarous, and uncultivated, ſtill ad-
hering to their old religion of wild, ro-
mantic, and legendary ſuperſtition, or rude
converts of Chriſtianity, relinquiſhing old
rites to graſp, with barbarian energy, the
ſuperficial principles of a new faith, that
at firſt ſoftened not their fierceneſs —
were the active ruling-ſpirits of the world.
From their homes in the primeval foreſts
of the North, this nomadic people overran
the lands of the more civilized but weaker

nations, then funk in enervating luxury from that ancient vigor, that made the matchlefs force of Roman arms, the glittering fplendor of Grecian enlightenment.

They defcended in countlefs hordes from their wild faftneffes of the North, bringing difmay and deftruction upon populous cities and wealthy, luxuriant lands. With a clafh like the rufh of a mountain torrent, the bands of the " yellow-haired Northmen " — the ftrong of limb, the dauntlefs and ruthlefs of heart — fwept all before them in their refiftlefs march, and returned to their homes laden with a wealth they knew not how to ufe, and clothed with favage terrors, more potent than even their favage arms, to break down the feeble refiftance of their weaker, though more civilized, fouthern neighbors. Over all the feas fwept the

armed ſhips of the Northmen, bound on
miſſions of piracy and rapine; no ſhore,
however remote, was ſafe from their at-
tacks, that had aught to tempt their cu-
pidity or love of martial deeds. Even
into the wild Northern Ocean they puſhed
their adventurous voyages,—diſcovered and
colonized the far-away iſland of Iceland;
and here, with charaćteriſtic energy, in
a climate that had ſo little to recommend
it as the habitation of man, they eſtab-
liſhed a republic, that for more than four
hundred years flouriſhed in its iſolated
liberty, and effećtually reſiſted the many
efforts of Norwegian princes to bring the
iſland under their deſpotic rule.

The hiſtory of this little Northern republic is full of wild and ſtrange romance,
and from its Sagas, wonderfully preſerved,
might be found material ſufficient to em-

ploy even the myriad romance-writers of this nineteenth century, without the fear of foon exhaufting the fupply.

From fome of thefe old ftories has been haftily and crudely conftructed the following tale, that, aiming not at literary excellence, only propofes to intereft, perhaps, a leifure hour, and call attention to this much-neglected field of romance. If this fhall be accomplifhed, the author will be repaid for thus venturing unannounced before the public.

THE AUTHOR.

CONTENTS.

Kormak.

CANTO I.

OGMUND.

CANTO I.

OGMUND.

NORTHMEN of old! 't was ye awoke the
world
From its lethargic flumber, — broke the reft
Of flumbering centuries, — when from forth
Your own rough Northern home ye poured the
flood
Of a wild enterprife, — an energy,
A will to do, — a wild and recklefs will,
That fwept like ftorm-wind o'er the ftartled world.

Northmen of old! 't was ye awoke the world
With your fhrill trumpet-notes; and where ye
came,
Your own ftrong fpirit filled the hearts of men:
They faw you landing, armed, upon their fhores,
From your light barges, with their brazen beaks:
Wild warriors of the North, they knew your fame,

And, leaping up from velvet couches, fled
From the wild torrent of your mountain fpears.
The element of action, kindling up
The heart, firing the brain, and making life
Leap, with the life-blood, through the boiling
    veins :
This wild, undaunted energy of foul
Bade ye, barbarian dwellers of the North !
Go forth, the pioneers whofe work fhould be
To kindle up, regenerate the world.
Your fluggifh neighbors of the lazy South
Caught infpiration from ye, as the garb
Of wealth and luxury, that made them weak,
Was rudely torn from off their trembling forms
By thofe who knew nor luxury nor fear.

    Northmen of old ! though wild and rude ye
      were,
Ye taught the feeble learning of the South
A ufeful leffon, that their wifeft fage,
Poring o'er volumes, wondrous-written tomes,
Had never dreamed of in his wifeft hour :
Your clafh of fteel proclaimed a mighty truth ;
And Northern fwords fpoke wifer than the pen.

    A cloud of romance hangs around old names.
The hero decks the favage of the North :
There is a charm in wild and recklefs deeds,

A thrilling fympathy with dauntlefs hearts ;
And gentle minds, while dwelling on the theme
Of the wild deeds of rapine and of war,
Still feel a kindly intereſt in thofe
Old hero-pirates of the early North.

Alone, in icy feas that gird it round,
A wintry belt, o'er which down from the pole
The frozen blaſt comes, claſhing like a knight
Clad in a cryſtal armor, war waging
'Gainst its lone, defencelefs ſhore, is Iceland.
Here, in old time, the rovers of the North
Planted their dwellings ; here, of old, they built
A rude republic : crude and rough indeed
As the wild beings, tribute of the fea,
Thrown like the fea-foam, gathered from afar,
Roughly upon the ſhore.   The wild fea-king,
Steered by his raven compafs to the iſle,
Soon learned to call it home ; and from that home,
His ice-bound fortrefs, ſhadowed by the North,
He turned adventurous beaks ; home again,
Wearied in conteſt both with man and fea,
Sailed his ſtorm-beaten barks ; when the white
        peaks
Of Iceland's mountains glittered o'er the fea,
Their frozen ſilence ſpoke to him of home :
And fmiled pale welcome to their daring fon, —
Their warlike fon, born of an ocean fire.

Flying from the oppreffion of his king,
From the fierce and iron rule of Harald,
The ftern tyrant of old warlike Norway,
Ogmund embarked his fortunes on the fea, —
His children and poffeffions, — and failed forth
To feek thofe lands that in the far Northweft
Had been discovered, that haply he might live
Free from the yoke that galled his lion fpirit ;
Willing to brave the dangers of new lands, —
Thofe vague, myfterious dangers, that hung
Like demon fpirits round the realms afar,
Frighting the fouls of fuch as knew of fear,
But not the foul of Ogmund : a brave heart
Was his inheritance from warlike fires ;
And not the perils of a ftormy fea,
Nor the rough wildnefs of a northern clime,
Where Ice and Winter rule the realm fupreme,
And fcarcely yield to Summer's milder fway, —
Could daunt the Northman's heart, — a heart
          inured
To war and danger from his days of youth.

Ogmund embarked for Iceland ; and at length,
After much danger on the ftormy fea,
He reached that ifland ; landed there his freight,
Himfelf, his children, and his houfehold goods ;
Pitched on a fpot where he might build his houfe,
And took poffeffion of the lands around,

Somewhat regardlefs of the prior claims
Of thofe firft fettlers, who fuppofed that they
Had better rights than the laft comer had.
But when the warlike Ogmund fought, and flew
A half a fcore of them, with a great fword,
An heirloom of his race, tall as himfelf,
And quite as little polifhed as its owner,
The firft poffeffors found that he had rights
They had not at the firft perceived, and fo
Left him to the enjoyment of their lands,
Rather than meet his heavy argument,
Which always filenced them.

                     But reftlefs ftill,
Ogmund would fometimes take a cruife at fea,
And meeting other roving, warlike fhips,
Would ftill indulge an old propenfity, —
And failing out with one fhip, would return
Sometimes with two.   And thus his name be-
       came
Well known and famous.   He grew in riches, —
A wealth of Iceland fields and herds and flocks.
And when at laft he died, advanced in years, —
Died quietly in his manfion, by the fea,
On which fo oft he perilled his wild life, —
He left behind a heritage of fame ;
And, what perhaps they valued more, riches
And fhips and large eftates, to his two fons.

Kormak and Thorgils were the fons of Og-
    mund ;
Kormak the elder, and inherited
The larger part of all the large eftates
Their warlike father had bequeathed to them,
With all that father's foul of recklefs daring,
And reftleffnefs, though foftened and adorned
By many graces, both of mind and perfon.
He was a fkilful fcald, framing his verfes
Sometimes relation of his father's deeds,
Though oftener telling of the beauty,
The countlefs charms, of fome Icelandic fair ;
And often, too, the youthful fcald would wage
A war of ftrophes with his poet friends :
His father vanquifhed neighbors with the fword ;
Kormak o'ercame them in the war of words.
Yet was he not unmindful of the gift, —
The laft great gift his dying father gave, —
The huge two-handed fword, with this advice :
" If you would win refpect from men, my fon,
Learn to ufe this ; 't will settle all debate,
Will make you honored, famous, wealthy, great ;
And be thy mark of rightful lineage too
From me, who in my youth received this blade
From my brave fire, my only heritage."
And Kormak learned to ufe the famous fword :
And there were none, of all the youths around,
Who could compete with him and his great fword.

A handfome youth was Kormak, tall and ftrong,
As ftraight and firm as ftands the Norway pine
In the old land from which his father came.
His raven hair hung round a dauntlefs brow,
And eyes that challenged all who met their gaze ;
Yet had their kindling glances generous warmth
When fofter feelings moved him. He was loved
Of many friends, and firft of thefe was Thorgils,
His younger brother ; for between the two,
Although diffimilar, was a ftrong love,
So great that their two hearts feemed only one ;
And it became a faying in the land,
When they would picture friendfhip ftrongly :
" Closely knit in kindred love as Kormak
And his brother Thorgils." Yet all unlike
Were they in mind and perfon ; for Thorgils
Was as gentle as his brother fiery :
A flender boy, with golden hair, and eyes
Of feminine foftnefs ; a voice as fweet
As a young girl's ; a winning gentlenefs
Had he, that feized upon the heart, and there
Enfhrined itfelf, as though there was its home.
Yet did he not lack manhood, for he was
Born of a race that knew not how to fear.
Companion with his brother at all times,
In all adventures, both by land and fea ;
For they inherited their father's love
Of feamanfhip, and were as much at home

Upon the deck of their fwift-failing bark
As when they rode or clambered o'er the hills
Of their wild, icy, northern mountain home.

"Brother," faid Kormak, as one eve they fat
Together near the fire in the great hall,
"I have a tale to tell you : Thou doft know
Three days ago I galloped o'er the hills,
To fee how fared our herdsmen in the west.
The fky was clear ; but ere the clofe of day
The fky was blackened with the heavy clouds,
That ftill grew darker, and obfcured the fun.
I knew a ftorm was hanging in thofe clouds :
The air was ftill and heavy, and no breath
Of wind was ftirring, as I croffed the hills
On my way homeward. Raven flew along,
And promifed with his fpeed to bring me home
Ere the wild war of elements began.
As I came near to Gnupsdale, dafhing on
With recklefs fpeed, quick came a flafh of light,
That almoft blinded me, and with that flafh
Came the loud crafh of thunder, its wild roar
Burfting low down, almoft upon my head.
Raven fprung wildly, madly, in the air,
And then, bewildered, stopped, and, fnorting,
        reared,
As though he battled with the ftorm above;
Another inftant, and a fecond crafh

Burst on our ears; the glaring sheet of flame,
The deaf'ning roar that mingled with the glare,
Maddened the frighted steed, and blinded him;
Backward he fell, as though the bolt had struck,
And horse and rider rolled upon the ground.
And now the wind came roaring, sweeping past,
As though that crash had loosed its brazen gates;
And floods of rain came, like a deluge, down,
Dashed in wild torrents on the trembling earth.
I gained my feet, and raised my frightened steed,
Whose quivering limbs, and drooping neck, and
     eye
With fear dilated, told his soul was tamed
By the wild terrors of the elements,
Loosed from the laws that bind their fearful
    strength.

" I sought the shelter of the nearest roof.
Gnupsdale was near; I could not choose but seek
E'en that protection from the raging storm.
I knew its owner was our father's foe,
But deemed him kinder than the foe without.
My horse was housed, and I beside the fire
Sat down, to dry my garments soaked with rain.
The fire burned brightly and my hosts were kind,
And soon I thought not of the storm without.
Gnupsdale, you know, is an estate of Thorkell,
But he resides at Tunga: this I knew,

And, knowing it, I thought to meet alone
Dependents, or perchance his kinfmen, there.
But while I fat befide the blazing fire
There came a fair-haired lady to my fide,
And bade me welcome to her father's hall, —
Bade me forget the ftorm that drove me there,
And gently offered reft and kindly cheer.
I ftammered thanks, — I knew not what I faid;
So fair a maiden I had never feen:
Her eyes were gentle, and her golden hair
Shone like a halo round her beauteous face.
She afked me if my fall had done me harm:
As in a dream, I vaguely anfwered, No; —
And other things fhe kindly, gently faid;
And bidding me once more a welcome kind,
Withdrew, and left me ftill as in a dream.

  "The ftorm was o'er. I fought my horfe again,
And galloped homeward, through the dark'ning
          night;
But ftill before me was that lovely face:
I faw naught elfe, and fince that hour have
          known
No thought but of her beauty and her grace.
I could not reft, and fo again to-day
To Gnupsdale went, to proffer her my thanks
For the fafe fhelter, and her greeting kind.
They coldly faid, at morn that fhe had gone

With her fire, Thorkell, and a numerous train,
Her brothers and her kinfmen, back to Tunga.

" Brother, it may be weaknefs, but I feel
A new emotion kindling in my heart :
I feel a reftleffnefs, a ftrange defire
To look again upon that beauteous face,
To hear that gentle voice, and meet again
The kindly glances of her heavenly eyes.
Is this not love ?   You oft have heard me fay
How vain and foolifh are a lover's fighs, —
That my free heart fhould never bend, and fue
For love or favors at a woman's feet.
Nay, do not fmile : my heart is furely won ;
And man muft yield to the decrees of fate."

And Thorgils, mufing filently awhile,
Thus anfwered him : " Kormak, liften to me ;
And though the tale I tell be one
That you have often heard, yet it is one
That it is well you now fhould think upon.
When firft our father fought this ifland fhore,
Thorkell dwelt here, upon the very fpot
Where now we dwell ; our father fettled near,
But foon difputes arofe between the two.
Our father, Kormak, was a daring man,
Taught in the fchool of action and of war :
He ever held the rule, that ' might is right,'

And made men yield before his iron will.
Thorkell was proud, and would not yield his
　　　lands,
His place, his power, unto a ſtranger's hand;
And ſo a mutual feud aroſe, and oft
From angry words they came to angry blows.

" Our father made a voyage to Norway once,
And, driven by a wild and fearful ſtorm,
His ſhip was wrecked amid the Orkney Iſles.
The news came home to Iceland that his ſhip
Was wrecked at ſea, and all on board were loſt.
Then Thorkell, thinking that his ſtubborn foe
Could never come to trouble him again,
Summoned his friends around him, and rode
　　　forth
To wreak his vengeance on our father's friends.
They burned our houſe; they ſlew our faithful
　　　friends ;
They ſeized our goods; drove off our flocks
　　　and herds.
A truſty ſervant fled with you and me,
And placed us ſafe beyond fierce Thorkell's rage.
He thought we died within our blazing houſe,
And, grimly muttering, ' Thus my foes I cruſh,'
Turned joyful homeward, thinking Ogmund's
　　　race
Could never ſtand before his path again.

"A year paſſed on: one morning in the bay
Anchored two ſhips. Our father had returned.
What words can paint the rage that filled his
     breaſt,
When he beheld the ruins of his home!
Quickly he landed with his armed force,
And, learning who had dared to do this deed,
He led his followers ſwiftly here to Mel.

"Thorkell, when he beheld our father's flag
Floating upon the maſts of either ſhip,
Summoned his friends and ſervants all in haſte;
For now he ſaw the dead returned to life,—
The ſea had yielded up her daring ſon:
His ancient foe had come in arms and ſtrength
To pay his vengeance for a deadly wrong.

"Here, on the ſlope before this houſe of Mel,
They met and fought. It was a deadly ſtrife:
Our father fought, avenging his deep wrongs;
And Thorkell fought for ſafety, for his life.
The chieftains met; and each defiance hurled
Back on the other, as they madly ruſhed,
And claſhed their blades together. Our father
Was famed the boldeſt ſoldier of his time;
And Thorkell, too, was known for ſtrength and
     ſkill,
And a bold heart, that never quailed to fear.

Our father, though his fhield was cleft in twain,
And his proud creft was fhorn of floating plume,
Cut Thorkell downward, with a fweeping blow
That ftretched the warrior, bleeding, on the earth.
His friends were fcattered, flain, or wounded fore;
But one true friend his mafter's body begged,
And, Ogmund granting, bore it from the field.

" Then Ogmund took poffeffion of the lands
And the eftates of Thorkell, save Gnupsdale,
Which he gave to Thorkell's fons.   Here they
          bore
Their wounded father, as they thought, to die;
But Thorkell's wound at length in time was cured:
He journeyed northward, and foon gained new
          lands, —
Larger eftates than thofe that he had loft, —
By a rich marriage with the only child
Of old Bajarni, famed for wealth and lands, —
The richeft man who dwelt upon our ifland.

" This is the feud between our houfe and hers:
She you have feen at Gnupsdale is daughter
To Thorkell, whom of old our father fought.
Steingerda may be gentle, but her friends,
Her father, brothers, kinfmen, all her houfe,
Still hate our father, even in his grave:
They ftill hate us, his fons, heirs of that wealth

Which once was theirs, but which our father
  took, —
A rightful vengeance for the wrongs he bore.
You muſt indeed poſſeſs a valiant heart
(As well I know you do) even to hope
For love or favor from this hoſtile race,
Sprung from our father's ancient deadly foe.
Steingerda knew you not for Ogmund's ſon,
Or elſe, perchance, her greeting then had lacked
The cordial welcome that ſhe gave to you :
When ſhe ſhall know you as your father's ſon,
Her eyes will loſe their gentle, kindly glance,
And in its place will come the ſtony look
We ſaw in Thorkell, when we met at End,
And when that chieftain knew us at a glance
For ſons of Ogmund, and looked death at us.
Baniſh the thought, my brother, from your breaſt
Of loving her, from whom but hate is due ;
So ſhall you win repoſe of mind and heart ;
So ſhall you ſhun regrets that come too late."

"All this, dear Thorgils, has my own mind ſaid:
Thus has it counselled ; yet, in ſpite of all
That reaſon, judgment, or your love adviſe,
I feel a reſtleſs, wild deſire to ſeek
This maiden, even in her father's hall, —
To daſh aſide obſtructions that ariſe,
And prove a love that nothing can withſtand, —

A courage that ſhall bend e'en fate itſelf,
Compelling deſtiny to yield to me.
Say not that this is madneſs : there's a charm
In very reckleſſneſs that ſtill allures,
And conquers judgment in the daring heart.
Do not adviſe me more : to-morrow morn
Alone I go, diſguiſed as wandering minſtrel,
To ſeek Steingerda, — to brave her father, —
And follow this adventure to the end."

" That ſhall you not ! " Thorgils in haſte re-
          plied ;
" Think you ſo meanly of my father's ſon,
That he will lazily repoſe him here ?
Think you ſo poorly, brother, of my love ?
I go with you ! come weal, come woe, come death,
There is my place, brother, beſide you ſtill."

" Nay, Thorgils, I would rather go alone ;
But if you muſt, I will not ſay you nay :
We'll ſhow old Thorkell that a ſavage look
Has not the power to awe brave Ogmund's ſons ;
We'll ſhow that chief that enterpriſe ſtill lives,
And courage died not in our father's ſtock
When Ogmund died.   We owe it to our name
To ſhow the world our father's ſons are we.
Yet I am plunging you in dangers, Thorgils,
Fooliſhly, vainly, — you I ſhould proteċt :

My younger brother, whom our father gave
Into my charge when his protection failed,
And bade me keep you with my ftronger arm
From every danger.   No! you must not go;
Alone, I fhall not know what 't is to fear,
But you with me, my heart would fear for you,
And coward palenefs blanch my manly cheek."

But Thorgils, too, could be refolved and firm,
For no perfuafion could induce him ftay;
And fo it was refolved that they fhould go
Difguifed to Tunga, there to act as chance
And time fhould offer, or events compel.

Kormak.

CANTO II.

THE MINSTREL.

CANTO II.

THE MINSTREL.

CIRCLES the year! and when the finking fun
Shines cold and diftant on the freezing earth:
When Winter comes, clad in an icy garb,
Still hurried on by winds that wildly roar:
When the broad fields, fo lately green and glad,
Blighted beneath the feafon's frofty touch,
Wrap filent round them their white robe of fnow,
And, defolate and dreary, wait for Spring;
When the dark foreft fheds its leafy coat,
And the ftript branches, dreary fkeletons,
Stand fpectre-like, or wave in difmal gloom,
Creaking and moaning in the icy wind;
When the houfed products of the fruitful year
Promife fecurity from cold and want,
And crackling fires blaze brightly on the hearth,
And kindly friends are cluftered round the board;

We welcome Chriftmas! as an old, dear friend,
We give it fmiling welcome. What though Time
Has fwept away another year of life!
How many bleffings with the days have come!
How many mercies, comforts, joys, and hopes!
A year has paffed fince Chriftmas laft was here:
A year full crowded with events and acts,
With thoughts and memories, once awakened,
That never more can fleep. The thoughtful mind
Finds food for contemplation, as arife
The varied pictures of the clofing year;
Unwritten hiftories come crowding faft,
And forms and faces that have paffed away
Are mingled with them in the dreamy thought.
The facred influence of the holy birth
Awakes the reverent feelings of the heart;
But Memory, ftartled in the dreaming brain
By merry laugh and fmiling friends around,
Forgets to think upon the filent paft,
Under the noify influence of the hour.

Back from the prefent to the days of old!
From our blithe Chriftmas to the feaft of Jul!
From the religion of the lowly born
To the dark age when Odin's worfhip was!
In Tunga's halls, upon the Mother-night,
They feafted joyous, and the ample board
Groaned 'neath the weight of rich and generous
        cheer.

Affembled here were friends and kinfmen; all
Who claimed relation with old Thorkell's houfe
Came here this night to hold the annual feaft,
And wafte the hours until the morning's dawn
With feftal revelry, with waffail, fong and wine.

The banquet-hall, though rough and rudely
    built,
Was large and lofty, and the arching roof
Of rough-hewn timber fpanned full forty feet,
While twice that fpace meafured its utmoft length.
In brazen fockets fixed along the wall
On either fide a fcore of torches blazed,
Throwing a bright but flickering light around,
While gleamed their light on fhield and fword
    and fpear,
Hung in profufion on the lofty wall.
Beneath, along an oaken table ranged,
Sat the wild feafters of this night of Jul:
The drinking-horns from hand to hand paffed
    round,
Oft filled from the huge flagons on the board.

A platform, raifed two fteps above the floor,
Stretched from one end a fpace of thirty feet,
And here with tapeftry the walls were hung,
And richer garnifhed with their warlike gear:
Rich fuits of mail, and fwords inlaid with gold,

And axes, on whofe polifhed helves fhowed white
The luftrous gleaming of bright filver rings;
Banners, the trophies of the well-fought field;
And in the centre, from a brazen beak,
Captured in fome wild battle on the fea,
Hung a rich canopy, beneath which sat
In regal ftate the mafter of the feaft.
A tall old man was Thorkell, filver-haired,
And bent with age; but ftill within his eye
Shone the proud glance that age can never tame.
He wore a robe of velvet, richly wrought;
And, fpite of age, the chieftain's look was bold,
As well befeemed his ftate, — a feudal prince.
On Thorkell's left hand fat his youthful dame,
Through whom his rich eftates had come to him,
And Steingerda, his daughter, famed for beauty,
The faireft maiden of that northern ifland;
And other ladies, friends and kindred, graced
With their fair prefence and bright fmiles the
          board.
Upon the right the fons of Thorkell fat,
Loptur and Alf; the kinfmen of the houfe
Were ranged beyond, while on the lower floor
Sat the retainers, the well-tried foldiers,
Captains of veffels, petty officers,
Clofe feated all around the feftal board.
In rich, half-warlike, holiday attire,
They came to revel at their chieftain's feaft.

The Saxon face, the flashing Norman eye,
Spoke the wild, daring heart that filled each
    breast.

Behind the chair of Thorkell Narfi stood,
His chiefest councillor, though still a youth.
Full of quips and witty sayings was he,
Yet shrewd withal, advising prudently
To his too fiery and impetuous master,
Who gave to him alone the liberty
To curb his anger, or restrain his rage; —
A slender youth, with small and sparkling eyes,
A keen, quick look of satire and of craft,
Masked with a smile, — an ever-ready smile,
That lighted up his pale, but handsome face;
So gayly drest, he blazed with gold and gems.
Ever beside his master was he found,
Filling the golden cup that Thorkell held,
But seldom drinking of the wine he poured;
With easy grace on Thorkell's shoulder leaned,
Whispered and chatted gayly in his ear,
Launching some bolt of wit, that hit the mark,
And won the applause of merriment around.

Now from the outer door a butler came,
To ask his master if an aged minstrel,
Who craved admittance there, might be allowed
To sing a ballad of a former age,

And, with his little ſkill, do all the grace
Within his art to the high feſtival.
An old man, with long locks of ſilver hair
His tall form bent, a trembling ſtep of age,
His right hand leaning on a fair-haired boy,
The other reſting on an oaken ſtaff,
The minſtrel entered.   But ere yet he reached
One half the diſtance to the upper hall,
Two viſitors arrived, who came in haſte,
And, preſſing paſt the old man, quickly ſtood
By Thorkell's ſide, who greeted them with joy,
And eagerly received the news they bore.
Theſe were two brothers, Oddur and Gudmund,
Sons of Thorveiga, whoſe wild forceries
And oracles had given to her the fame
Of mind familiar with the *evil god*,
And power, through him, to propheſy what time
Had ſhrouded darkly in a future age;
And theſe, reputed as her ſons, who dwelt
With her in her ſecluded hut, — her ſtrange,
Wild ſervitors, — were men of giant forms,
Rude in their manners, clumſy in their gait,
Ill-looking faces, where deceit and fraud
Mingled with coarſeneſs and ſtupidity;
Great brutes they were, ſo huge and ſtrong,
And ſullen in their looks, that a ſhudder —
Not fear, but loathing — paſſed around the hall.
Thorkell bade Nari find them each a place;

Then, rifing, thus addreffed his guefts, who ceafed
Awhile their revelry, and liftened as
The old man fpoke, with earneft voice, and eye
That flafhed in fiercenefs when his paffions woke.

"I need not tell to you, my friends, the wrongs
I bore from Ogmund; thefe you know too well.
The robber now is dead, and unavenged
Are all the injuries he did to me.
The wealth he took his fons inherited,
And now enjoy.   I fwore a facred oath
To wreak my vengeance dearly on the fire;
He has efcaped me, but the fons remain.
And now I fwear, by Thor, and Odin too,
Here, on this facred, honored Mother-night,
To fweep the race of Ogmund from the earth,—
To fhed each drop of blood that now doth flow,
Kindred to him, in any heart that beats
On this our ifland.   You, my friends, I truft
To give me aid of arms and valiant hearts.
The fons of Ogmund boast of many friends,
And Kormak feeks to win a fame for arms
And daring deeds; but you fhall fcatter them
Like driving foam before the ocean wind,
And boaftful Kormak fhall go feek his fire, —
Shall bear my vengeance paft the filent gate
To that dead foe; not even death fhall fave
From my fierce vengeance, nurfed through many
        years,

That thus at laft in blood it may be drowned.
Thorveiga, who did never fpeak in vain,
Communing with the gods, bids me go on,
And victory fhall crown our undertaking.
Give me your anfwer! fhall I have your aid,
Freely and boldly, in this juft emprife ?
Or do you fear young Kormak's boafted fword?"

And now arofe a wild, tumultuous din ;
Swords were clafhed, and cries of " Death to
    Kormak ! "
Shook e'en the maffive timbers of the hall, —
Made the red torches flicker their wild light,
And ruftled fwords and axes on the wall.
A wild, fierce joy fprung up in Thorkell's eye ;
Already he beheld his proftrate foes,
And drank the deep, the long-delayed revenge.
When now the filence was at length reftored,
He thanked his wild retainers for their zeal,
And promifed foon to bring them to the deed.

Meantime the aged minftrel and the boy,
His harp-bearer, had refted on the bench
That ftood againft the wall ; filent they fat,
Yet once their eyes had met, and then there
    glanced
A look of quick intelligence between,
Though none had marked it 'mid the ftirring
    fcene

And the wild tumult that fo fhook the hall.
But now, remembered, Thorkell bade them come
Still nearer, and that Narfi bear a bowl
Of wine to the old man, which was declined ;
Then, bending o'er his harp, the minftrel fung.
With faltering hand at firft the chords he preffed,
In trembling tones at firft his voice was heard,
But, fired at length by the wild foul of fong,
In ftrength and richnefs grew the fwelling tones.

" When Harald Harfagra was king,
    And fat on Norway's throne
('T was Harald made the kingdom his,
    And all the power his own),

" There dwelt at the court of Harald,
    An Earl, who claimed that he
From the ancient kings of Norway
    Could trace his pedigree.

" He won the favor of Harald
    By bending to his will,
And the king endowed him richly
    With lands and wealth, until

" His caftles he counted by fcores,
    And fhips like flocks that fly
Of the white-winged, failing fea-birds
    Amid the ocean fky.

" But dearer than caſtles on land,
　　Ships upon the water,
　A richer boon than e'en Harald's love
　　Was his only daughter.

" Fair as the gleam of the funſhine
　　When morning greets the ſight,
　As the golden ſun, upriſing,
　　Rolls round 'mid crimſon light.

" Fairer than words can picture her,
　　Fairer than tongue can tell,
　As fair as the dead we cheriſh,
　　Within our hearts that dwell.

" While war was raging around her
　　(The life of man was war),
　The heart of the maid was gentle
　　As light of evening ſtar.

" She ſhuddered to think of battle,
　　Yet felt her pulſes ſtart
　When they told ſome deed of daring,
　　Some deed of dauntleſs heart.

" And the maid had many ſuitors ;
　　Her beauty and her grace
　Won the hearts of thoſe old warriors,
　　A rude and ſavage race.

" And many a reckleſs ſoldier
 Within his mailed breaſt
Had often breathed a ſtifled ſigh
 His lips had ne'er confeſſed ;

" And many who went to battle,
 As their wild war-cries roſe,
Breathed ſoft the name of the maiden,
 And daſhed againſt their foes.

" They recked not of death or danger,
 For a wilder ſtrife by far
Had raged in their ſteel-clad boſoms,
 Than ever raged in war.

" But Skeggi, a famous warrior,
 And rich in ſhips and land,
Was ſtill a conſtant wooer
 For gentle Unna's hand.

" And he won her father's favor,
 Who bade his daughter ſee
In Skeggi a fitting huſband,
 For ſhe his wife muſt be.

" But the maiden mourned in ſecret,
 Mourned with a grieving heart,
For ſhe could not love the warrior,
 And oft her tears would ſtart, —

"Would ſtart as ſhe thought of another,
    A gentle, gallant youth,
To whom ſhe had pledged in ſecret
    Her heart in maiden truth.

"But her lover was poor, and yet
    He had not won a fame,
And her father laughed at the ſtripling,
    A youth without a name.

"But the heart of a dauntleſs race
    Beat in his youthful breaſt,
And he vowed to win the maiden,
    Or death ſhould be his reſt.

"And Unna told her father
    How he had won her heart,
But the Earl was proud, and bade her
    From this weak love to part.

"With her tears ſhe ſought to move him,
    But he coldly turned away,
And, true to his word with Skeggi,
    He fixed her wedding-day.

"At length the fatal day arrived,
    The day when ſhe muſt wed
The huſband her ſire had choſen, —
    She wiſhed that ſhe was dead.

" In the hall were hung the banners,
 A rich and gallant fhow,
And Skeggi was flufhed and joyous,
 But Unna white as fnow.

" The Earl had filled up a goblet
 Of rich and fparkling wine:
'I drink,' cried he, 'to thee, Skeggi!
 Now thou art fon of mine.'

" But ere he had drained the goblet,
 There came a rufhing found,
That ftartled the guefts affembled,
 And fhook the flags around.

" That rufhing found came fweeping on
 Like fwell of ocean wave,
And Skeggi felt his ftrong heart tremble,
 That heart he thought fo brave.

" Through opening doors a tide rufhed in,
 Of men and fteel that tide;
Fair Unna's heart leaped up how wildly, —
 Her lover, by her fide,

" Led on that band to win the maid,
 Or, true to plighted word,
Lay down his life before the hazard,
 The hazard of the fword.

" The clafh of fteel rung wild and high,
  And poured a crimfon flow, —
Libations of the heart's red wine
  Fell on the floor below.

" Through blood and ftrife the maid was borne
  From that wild fcene away,
Fainting, within her lover's arms
  A helplefs burden lay.

" They gained the fhore, the bark was launched,
  Quickly they fpread the fail,
The fleeteft fhip of all the North
  Was foon before the gale.

" Behind them came a thoufand foes,
  The fea with fails was white,
Like the fwift fea-bird on they flew,
  And vanifhed in the night.

" Thus Skeggi loft his lovely bride,
  And yet, throughout the night,
He ftill failed on ; at morning's dawn
  There was no fail in fight.

" Weary and fad, he turned his bark,
  Homeward he fteered his way,
And often curfed in bitternefs
  That darkly-ending day.

"And thus the youth the maiden won;
    He bore her fouthward far,
And in new lands he gained a name
    By valiant deeds in war.

"But dearer than the name he gained,
    Dearer than all befide, —
Than wealth and honors, that were his, —
    Was his fair Norfeman bride.

"And many fons were born to him,
    Inheriting his fame :
Beft known of thefe throughout the North
    Was Ogmund's famous name."

Thus far the minftrel fung; but with the name,
The hated name of Ogmund, there arofe
A found of tumult wild throughout the hall,
And darkening brows and angry eyes were bent
On the old harper, while his voice was drowned
In their loud, angry murmurs : for Skeggi
Was Thorkell's fire, and fuch a tale as this
Was all unfuited to the time and place.

On Thorkell's brow was feen tne flufh of rage;
He bade his fervants break the minftrel's harp,
And bear the old man and the boy away,
And lock them in the vaults beneath the hall,

Till he might judge what punifhment was due
For their rafh deed.   The old man's harp was
        feized,
And dafhed in pieces at his very feet.
His tall form ftraightened, and his eye flafhed
        fire, —
One ftep he took, as though his age was loft
In the fierce infult, but the boy advanced,
And, with a whifpered word, reftrained him ;
Then, with downcaft eyes and trembling ftep,
They led him from the hall.   But once he turned,
And caft a glance of hate and menace round,
At which they only fcoffed ;   and Narfi cried :
" The old man's angry that we did not choofe
To praife his finging ;   or he fears the cold,
Damp vault may fpoil the fweetnefs of his voice."
But Thorkell bade him hold his peace, for much
It chafed him that the praife of Ogmund's race
Should thus have founded in his banquet-hall.

Kormak.

CANTO III.

THE ESCAPE.

CANTO III.

THE ESCAPE.

G UDRIDA, Thorkell's dame, had left the
feaſt,
And Steingerda and all the lady gueſts
Attended her; as wilder grew the ſcene
Each moment, for the red, bright, ſparkling wine
Uſurped fair Reaſon's throne within each brain.
Thorkell withdrew, for age, with iron hand,
Had cruſhed in him the power, that once was his,
To revel with the wildeſt, and prolong
Through midnight to the dawn the mad carouſe.
The revel ſtill grew wilder; all reſtraint
Was now caſt off, and each abandoned him
To the wild genius of the feſtal night.
The mingling voices of an hundred gueſts
Were raiſed together, and in diſcord oft;
And then again thoſe maſſive caſtle-walls
Seemed reeling inward with the wild refrain,

4

As some old song or festal glee was sung,
And each one joined with fierce and frantic zeal.

Narfi was seated in the chair of state,
Where Thorkell late had sat; and he alone
Of all the feasters in that banquet-hall
Was not bewildered or o'erpowered with wine.
With meditative face, shading his eyes
With his white hand, he sat, observing all
That chanced around, but quite unmoved and
    calm
Amid a tumult might have waked the dead.
And thus, thought he, men seek for happiness:
"O weak and brainless fools! what joy is there
In thus degrading man below the brutes!
Taking away from him the only thing,
His reason, that makes him better than the herds
Of grazing cattle, wand'ring o'er our hills! —
But soft! I see before me many men
Of wisdom greater than I dare to claim:
Men of sound minds, of strong and earnest
    thought —
And am I better than all these I see
Thus drowned and stupefied in this red wine?
Or is there magic in your ruby stream,
Enchanting, with a deadly serpent power,
Your trembling captives, while you drink their
    blood,

Changing the godlike mind to worthleſs droſs !"
As thus he thought, and from a flagon poured
Its ſparkling contents on the oaken floor,
His mind reverted to the minſtrel's ſong ;
And long he pondered, till a ſudden thought
Flaſhed on his brain : riſing, he ſeized a torch,
And bent his ſteps toward the vaults that lay,
Dreary and dark, beneath the banquet-hall.

A narrow room — eight paces in its length
By four in breadth, the walls and floor of ſtone,
The ceiling timber, and the door of oak —
Confined the minſtrel who had dared to ſing
The praiſe of Thorkell's foe before that chief,
And the fair boy, his harp-bearer, who ſhared
His fortunes in the cold and dreary cell.
Againſt the wall, upon the other ſide
Of the long corridor, from which the vaults
Had entrance, thoſe who brought the captives
          here
Had placed a torch, whoſe flickering light
Shone faintly through the narrow open ſpace
Above the door, and traced againſt the wall
And on the floor the croſſings of the bars
That ſpread their iron network over it,
Admitting air and the faint, ſtruggling light.
No bed, no ſtraw, nothing but naked walls
And damp, cold floor ! It was a dreary place

To pafs a night; and the uncertainty
Of how much longer time their fate to ftay
Within its walls made it feem ftill more drear.

Their jailers gone, the minftrel with a ftart
Sprung up erect, and paced with rapid ftrides
The narrow room.   His hands were clenched
          in rage,
And all the paffions he had fmothered down
Now woke to fury in his heaving breaft.
Calm and ferene the boy looked on, unmoved
By all the tempeft of his rage, until,
Its wild burft o'er, the minftrel grew more calm;
And then the boy advanced toward him,
And, placing one hand on his fhoulder, faid:
" Paffion is idle; for the fong you fung
Was fung in daring, to awake their rage, —
You knew the vengeance of an angry foe
Would fall on you, and recklefs braved that rage.
Now, Kormak, do not wafte your energy
In hurling curfes, which can do no harm
To thofe at whom you aim; but let us fee
How beft we can difpofe to pafs the night
In thefe poor lodgings; for fome fleep we 'll need,
And with to-morrow may come ftirring fcenes."

Kormak put one arm round his brother's neck,
Looking in his calm, gentle eyes, he faid

"Your brave, ftrong heart, dear brother, tells
        to me
How much more manly you are than I am;
While I in paffion rage and fret myfelf,
Wafting my energy and ftrength and time,
You calmly think, — are always ftill unmoved:
But when the time for ftirring action comes, —
When danger threatens, — then a lion heart
Speaks out in daring from thofe gentle eyes.
In time of danger I am fearlefs too,
But cannot curb my paffion, nor reftrain
Impatience or defire, as you, dear brother, can."

    And now they talked of all had chanced that
        night, —
Of Thorkell's enmity; how their mad freak
Had placed them in his power; and what their
        fate,
If he fhould learn who they, his captives, were.
But no figh or vain regret they uttered:
Spoke in all calmnefs of the coming morn,
And meafured all their chances for efcape.
And Kormak, too, found time to fpeak again
Of fair Steingerda, — her grace, her beauty:
Not e'en reflecting that her luftrous eyes
Had been the lure to this their ftrange mifhap;
Or, if the thought occurred, his heart leaped up,
And welcomed everv danger for her fake.

Now, in one corner of their dreary cell,
Upon their cloaks the brothers laid them down,
And foon, in fpite of danger, cold, or e'en
Of anxious thoughts, they loft themfelves in
    fleep.
At times the muffled founds above their heads
Waked them a moment, and they fell afleep
Again, with faint confcioufnefs of waking.

When Steingerda had left the banquet-hall,
She fought her chamber; but the founds that
    came
Wild from below forbade the thought of fleep.
Seated befide the fire, unconfciously
Her thoughts turned to the minftrel and his
    fong;
And much fhe dwelt upon the fearful hate
That urged her father to a fierce revenge
On Ogmund's fons, for wrongs done by their
    fire;
And then the form of Kormak came before
Her meditative mind, — and well fhe knew
There was no hatred in her heart toward him;
For fhe had learned at length, when he was gone,
That it was Kormak who had been her gueft
That eve at Gnupsdale; and fince then her
    thoughts
She often found returning to the youth,

Recalling thofe few words he faid to her.
And now the minftrel and her evening gueft,
In fpite of her, engroffed her thoughts, and
    came
Always together, mingling in her mind.
At length the thought occurred to her to feek
The vault where Thorkell had imprifoned him,
And queftion the old bard, why he had fung
The fong that fo excited Thorkell's rage.
She called her maid ; the girl, quite overcome
With wearinefs, in fpite of all the founds
That thundered ftill below, had fallen afleep :
So, taking up her lamp, and throwing on
A heavy cloak, — for the night air was cold, —
She went alone toward the dungeon vaults.

He who had feen her as fhe paffed along,
So filent and fo fair, through thofe rude halls,
Her beauty half unfeen, and yet augmented,
By the faint glimmer of her fluttering light,
Might well have thought fome Peri of the air
Had left her home amid the realms of light,
To do a good deed for weak, erring man. —
Yet oft within the faireft forms are found
The fouls leaft beauteous ; — for curiofity,
Or woman's light caprice, Steingerda fought
Her father's captives at this lonely hour ;
Or perchance the adventure of the act

Had lured her to it ; but not that holy thought
That bids the gentle heart to thofe that mourn
Go offer confolation, urged her on.
She had a foft and kindly woman's heart,
That would not do a cruel act ; but yet
By her fair prefence in his lonely cell
She might inflict on that poor captive youth
A deeper wound than e'en her father's hate,
In all its fiercenefs, had the power to give.

    The bolts were drawn, the heavy key was
       turned,
And Narfi entered at the opening door ;
His glittering drefs contrafted with the walls,
Like diamonds flafhing in a leaden ring.
Still on the floor the minftrel and the boy
Were lying. Narfi held his torch above
Their heads, and with a fcrutinizing eye
Examined the appointments of their drefs,
And laft their faces ; Thorgils' gentle eye
Was bent, with look of childifh wonderment,
Upon his rich-apparelled vifitor,
And Narfi turned from him, well fatiffied
That he, at leaft, was only what he feemed, —
A very fimple boy, the harp-bearer.
But when he met the minftrel's eye, its flafh
Had more of youth than trembling age in it :
And his firm limbs, not wholly hid from view

Within his ample cloak, fhowed full and round,
And lacked the weak and fhrunken form of age.
A smile arofe on Narfi's fcornful lip,
As thus he found his firft fufpicion true.
Still as a ftatue, with his blazing torch
Throwing its full, red light on them, he ftood.
At length he fpoke : —

            " Minftrel, in vain you feek
To cover youth with age. Old you are not ;
Nor are you wandering minftrel, as you feem,
Though fomething of the minftrel's art is yours,
And you can fing a very ftirring fong.
And did you think to fing your father's praife
Here in thefe walls, the dwelling of his foe,
And pafs unharmed away ? Kormak, your fate
Is fealed ; and you will pay the penalty
Of death for this, your lateft, maddeft act.
And your young brother, in his home at Mel,
Shall foon be wakened with a ftorm of fteel ;
And all the wrongs done to our noble houfe,
By your bafe robber fire, in blood avenged."
Kormak fprung up, and dropped the fhrouding
       cloak
From off his agile limbs ; with flafhing eye
He anfwered him : " He was no robber, flave !
Back to your mafter ! tell him, that his foe
Hurls a defiance in his very teeth.

Think you my foul is tamed, becaufe my limbs
Are bound within this dungeon? Think it not:
No more I fear your mafter, Thorkell, now,
Than when he threatened what he could not do."
Narfi had drawn his fword when Kormak rofe,
But never moved a foot. "Wear out," he faid,
"Your few brief hours in curfing : thus alone
Have you the power to vent your rage on us;
For you are harmlefs as a hiffing fnake
Whofe fangs have been extracted. Now to fleep,
If fleep you can : to-morrow you muft die."

Narfi was gone ; his footfteps died away
In the long corridor, on the ftairway.
Once more the brothers laid them down to fleep
The few fhort hours till morn ; but once again
There came the found of footfteps, till at length
It ftopped before their door : the key was turned ;
Again the heavy door fwung grating back :
Ofwald, the jailer, entered, raifed his torch,
And looked around, and then paffed out again,
And Steingerda advanced. Kormak beheld,
But fcarce could deem the vifion real, fo fair
So dreamlike in her beauty the young girl
Stood, trying to pierce the gloom ; for her lamp,
Flickering in the doorway, gave faint light,
And Ofwald's torch was fhaded by the wall.
"Minftrel," fhe faid, "you braved my father's
        rage ;

Yet ftill, in pity for your age and art,
I fain would know why thus you dared to fing;
I fain would fhield you from the fate you
    fought."

" Fair lady," fpoke the minftrel, "you alone
Are caufe of this adventure ; for your love
The youth you fheltered from the raging ftorm
One eve at Gnupsdale, though your father's foe,
Has come to feek you in your father's hall ;
And, though death meet him, feel his heart
    repaid
By one bright fmile, one gentle look from thee."
And Kormak threw afide the filver hair,
His badge of age, and, kneeling at her feet,
Poured out his wild, paffionate heart of love,
With the rich eloquence that lovers have.
And Steingerda, amazed, bewildered, liftened,
While Kormak kiffed her hand, and uttered vows
That fcarce fhe heard in her bewilderment.
" But why awake my father's rage ?" fhe faid ;
" Wherefore your fong ?"
             " I heard them bafely fpeak
Of my brave father : they called him robber ;
My foul chafed at it ; but I could not fpeak
While my full heart was hiffing hot to tell,
That, when he lived, he taught them fairer
    fpeech,

But now, being dead, their coward lips were
    loofed
To flander him. I could not tell them this,
For my difguife; but when they bade me fing,
The thought came to me, that, in Thorkell's hall,
'Twere fome revenge to fing my grandfire's
    praife;
And hence my fong."
              " Your life is forfeited
The inftant that my father knows your name."

    " That gay-dreffed youth who ftood by
        Thorkell's chair
Has lately left us, threatening me with death.
He knows of my difguife; though how he
    gueffed
My name I cannot tell."
              Steingerda mufed,
But quickly faid: " If you to-morrow morn
Are found within thefe walls, no power can fave
You from my father's long-delayed revenge.
If that I dare releafe my father's foe,
Will you, for love of me, appeafe his wrath
By fuch conceffions, in your power to make,
As may at length extinguifh this fierce feud,
And in its place build up a friendfhip ftrong?"

    " For love of thee," Kormak replied to her,

"There's naught I will not do, fo honor
And my dead father's name, that now I bear
Proudly and bravely, fhall receive no ftain.
I were fo much lefs worthy of thy love,
If I could ftoop to aught unworthily :
I muft not tamper with my father's fame,
A heritage of honor or of fhame, —
Honor, if I keep it ftill unblemifhed,
But fhame, if I fhould fully his brave fhield
By act unworthy of my father's fon.
But that which one ftrong, earneft heart may do,
With aid of friends and youth and enterprife,
That will I do, to win a boon fo dear
As thy rich heart, fair lady.   But perchance
All this I fpeak in vain ; yet in my heart
There is a fanguine voice, and it tells me
I fhall not die to-morrow, — fhall efcape ;
If through thy kindly aid, then doubly dear
Will be thy image, fhrined within my heart."
Then Kormak took his brother by the hand,
And told the lady what a daring heart
Beat in that gentle, fair-haired, blue-eyed boy.

Ofwald ftood by, with wonder in his eyes,
To fee the aged minftrel thus transformed.
Fofter-brother to his gentle lady,
He held the true devotion of his life
Due to her fervice.   Now fhe turned to him :

"Ofwald," fhe faid, "my dear fofter-brother,
This captive minftrel is a youth I love,
And Thorkell has refolved upon his death.
Dare you conduct him from thefe walls to-night,
And fly with him, and this brave boy, ere dawn
Beyond my father's anger and his power?"
"For thee I'll dare whatever man may dare,
My lady," Ofwald anfwered.

      "Then away!
Make all arrangements for their inftant flight;
Saddle the horfes: fteeds of fwifteft foot
Select from all that ftable here to-night;
And fhould you borrow of my father's guefts,
The purpofe muft excufe for once the breach
Of hofpitality. Ufe urgent hafte,
For one hour later underneath this roof,
And there would be no hope for your efcape.
My father wakes at dawn; and well I know
That Narfi will not fleep till he has poured
The night's difcovery in his mafter's ear."
Ofwald was gone. "No longer muft I ftay,"
Steingerda faid; "wrong have I done to come
Here in the night, in fecret, to your cell;
Nor had I come, perhaps, if I had known
It was no aged minftrel whom I fought.
Wrong have I done to hear the words of love
Spoken by one my father hates the moft;
But my weak woman's heart is moved for you,

And thus I fhield you from my father's hate.
But hear me, Kormak : do not feek again
To ftir my father's rage againft yourfelf
By fuch wild deed as this ; for were I not
A renegade from him whom I fhould ferve,
Your fates were fealed : before to-morrow's fun
Sunk in the weft your fouls were with the dead."
And Kormak kiffed her hand again, while fhe
Threw o'er his neck the filken fcarf she wore,
And hurried from the cell ; but at the door
Half turned, to give a laft and farewell glance
To Kormak, kneeling ftill, as at the fhrine
Kneels Odin's rapt, adoring worfhipper.

When Narfi left the captives in their cell,
Dwelling on what had chanced, he firft returned
Unto the revellers ; but they were few
Who now remained awake.   Upon the floor,
'Mid fcattered goblets, and feats overturned,
And pools of wine, in ftupid fleep were feen
The mad caroufers of an hour ago.
Sleep had o'erwhelmed their wine-encumbered
        minds,
And in the midft of fong and fpeech they fell,
And as they fell they flept.   Narfi beheld
The changed appearance of the hall, and fmiled,
But ftayed not long ; the heated, o'er-breathed
        air.

The fumes of wine and ale, the long-drawn
    breaths
Of the deep, heavy sleepers, troubled him,
And he went forth, still thinking, as he passed
Into the night-air, of his discovery
Of Kormak, and still seeking for the clew
To his strange visit there: nor could he frame
Another purpose than his earliest thought.
He knew that Kormak had met Steingerda
At Gnupsdale, and much he feared more than
    once
Had been her visitor. Why came he here?
And why had he excited Thorkell's ire
By his mad song? This would not further love.
Himself less careless, he knew not what deeds
Might be performed for very recklessness,
And sought a reason for a reckless act.

Besides the hate he bore the captive youth,
In common with the wronged house of Thorkell,
There was another reason for his joy
In finding Kormak in the aged bard:
He loved Steingerda, though that love unknown
To all but his own heart; and ambition
Joined with love had been the leading motives
Guiding his action, ruling all his thoughts,
For many, many months; he knew himself
Full of stratagems, and had dared to hope

He might by thefe achieve the purpofed ends
Of both his paffions, — marry his miftrefs,
And win through her pofition. Now, thought
    he,
I can gain more of Thorkell's confidence
By this difclofure, at the fame time ftrike
A dangerous rival from my path of love:
Thus I advance ftill nearer to my ends.
The found of horfes' feet aroufed his thoughts;
Three horfemen came dim through the fhades
    of night,
And almoft rode on him. As he drew back,
The foremoft hailed him: "Ho, Sir Boafter!
    ftay,
And bear a meffage from me to your lord:
Tell him the minftrel could not wait for him,
But fends, inftead, his greeting. For yourfelf,
Learn not to threat; for boafting words are weak,
And often are as unfulfilled as thofe
You gave to me to-night. I may not ftay:
The lines of day are lighting up the eaft,
And time is precious; for you prophefied
This day fhould be my laft: and fo adieu!"
And Narfi faw the three dafh on again.
He ftood transfixed, gazing on vacancy
Where they had vanifhed; then, as the founding
Of their quick gallop died away, at length
The power of utterance came back to his tongue,

5

And through his clofe-fet lips he hiffed his curfe,
Its burning heat quenched by the cold night-air,
Upon their flight; in frenzy ftamped his foot
Upon the frozen earth, that took the blow
As little harmed by it as thofe he curfed
Were by the maledictions heaped on them.
His anger fpent, he turned toward the gate,
Queftioning in his mind by what ftrange means
The captives had efcaped.   Raifing his eyes,
He faw the gleaming of the light come down
From a high cafement in the lofty wall
Of the fquare tower upon the weftern side.
" My lady's lamp is burning late," he faid.
" Who was their jailer?   Ofwald!   All is clear!
Her fofter-brother fet her lover free!
That love is hopelefs, lady!   If not I,
At leaft not he fhall ever be thy lord!"
With upturned face and burning eyes he fpoke,
But the cold walls heard not his threatening
        words.
Confcious of weaknefs, confcious too of ftrength,
He fummoned all his art to guide his way,
Dark and obfcure, toward his deftined end.

Kormak.

CANTO IV.

BATTLE ISLE.

CANTO IV.

BATTLE ISLE.

THE winter months were paſt, — thoſe
    cold, long months
Through which the funſhine ſleeps, forgetting
    earth,
Or looking coldly and obliquely down ;
No loving warmth in even noontide beams,
No friendſhip in his rays. But awaking
From his long lethargy, at laſt the ſun
Began to climb the arch, and lift the veil
That hid his kindneſs from the eyes of men,
And ſhow himſelf again the genial god
Before whoſe face the tributary world
Arrays itſelf in verdure. The white robe
Of frigid Winter melted in his light ;
The faſt-bound ſtreams reſumed their rapid flow ;
Through the warm earth the little blades of graſs
Came forth ſo cautiouſly, as if in fear

The icy blaſts of winter might return
To kill their tender life ; the naked trees
Arrayed their hundred arms in leafy garb,
And drank the ſunbeams up. From milder
    climes
Came back the migratory flocks, that learn
By Nature's telegrams when the young Spring
Leaps to his ſeat, the ruler of the world,
And Winter melts in his cold ſnows away.
And in this northern clime a wondrous change
Came in a few bright days: the dreary world
Lay one day like the lifeleſs cryſalis,
The next arrayed itſelf in ſummer's hues, —
A butterfly, and like the butterfly,
Flaſhed gayly, brightly, through as brief a life.

There was an iſland with a rocky ſhore
Upon its northern ſide, where the high crags
Climbed up above the ſea a thouſand feet ;
Many an iceberg, floating from the north,
Had wrecked itſelf upon thoſe moveleſs rocks,
And ſhivered peak by peak, until the ſea
Was covered with a floating wreck of ice, —
The crumbled fragments of the frozen berg,
That once was vaſter than the iſland crags
On which its voyage was wrecked. A mile away
From the main ſhore of Iceland was the iſle ;
Though the wild, rocky ſhore was ſtrewn with ice

Through the whole year, yet, floping from the
      crags
Toward the fouth and weft, the other fhore
Caught the firft funfhine of the early Spring,
Put the firft verdure of the feafon on,
And fmiled fecure beneath the rocky wall.
It was a funny fpot, as fair and bright
As though it lay within a milder zone :
Here the huge pines rofe towering to the fky,
Clothed in their garb of an eternal green ;
While groves of birch-trees bent their graceful
      boughs
To the light airs breathed gently from the fouth ;
And the green grafs grew greener, frefher here
Than on the mainland fhore. No one dwelt here :
But oft in fummer parties came, and pitched
In this fweet fpot their tents, and whiled away
The days, forgetful that they lived fo near
The frozen regions of perpetual cold, —
The home of glaciers, and thofe northern feas,
Fixed, filent, motionlefs, congealed forever.

No one dwelt here ; yet 'mid the lofty pines
I fee white tents, and many moving forms :
Perchance fome idlers come to greet the Spring
In this fair fpot where firft fhe greets the earth.
Upon an open fpace, a grafly lawn,
Smooth as a carpet, floping to the weft,

And foft with verdure, the encampment ftood.
The pine-trees formed the back ; advanced from
      thefe,
Yet fcarce beyond their fhade, a group of tents,
With ftreamers gayly floating from their peaks,
Were cluftered.   On the right and on the left,
Two arrow-flights apart, were alfo fet
Two other groups of tents : feparate both,
Like little villages ; in each a tent
Higher than thofe around, in front of which
From a tall ftandard hung a blazoned flag :
The talleft ftandard ftood before the group
Of tents that formed the centre.   Armed men
·Were moving to and fro, and lances, fwords,
And fuits of mail flafhed brightly in the rays
Of the now fetting fun ; yet mixed with thefe
Were other forms, that wore no warlike mien :
For there were groups of ladies, gayly dreft,
Straying from tent to tent, watching the fun,
As in a crimfon glow his bright orb funk
Beneath the mainland's white-topped mountain
      heights,
Kindling their cold fnows with his lurid fire,
As he withdrew behind their ridgy wall ;
Or chatting gayly of the coming morn,
Or flirting, 'mid the birch-groves, with the
      youths
Who bore them company.   Thus evening paffed,

And night came down amid the dark-leaved
      pines,
And hufhed them all to filence and repofe.

When Thorkell learned that his moft hated foe
Had been within his power, and yet efcaped,
His rage o'erleaped all bounds: fiercely he hurled
On Narfi the torrent of his curfes ;
That artful youth in filence bent his head
Until the ftorm was paft ; nor did he fpeak
The thought within his heart, that Steingerda
Had given the means to fet the captives free :
He locked this fecret faft within his breaft,
Hoping to find a time when it might ferve
Some better fervice than it now could ferve ;
Nor did he deem it wife to bring the rage
Of Thorkell on the lady ; for he knew
That fhe would trace the thought back to its
      fource,
And he fhould bear the blame ; and then, befide,
He could not prove his fhrewd fufpicion true.
And now the long-nurfed plan in Thorkell's
      heart,
Of an armed vengeance, grew dearer to him ;
And all the preparation, muftering men,
Collecting arms, to make that vengeance fure,
Went brifkly on ; but fcarce a week had paffed,
When came a meffenger from Olaf Pa,

Whofe Thingfman Thorkell was, forbidding him
To march againſt his neighbor with armed men,
To plunge in war and blood the peaceful land
O'er which he claimed to rule. Thorkell at firſt
Bade Olaf's meſſenger return to him
Who fent him, with the anſwer, that he chofe
To bear no queſtion of his purpofed act, —
That he denied the right to interfere
To Olaf Pa, or any living man.
But Narfi calmed his maſter's boiling rage,
Showing him thus that he would bring himſelf
To certain ruin; and counfelled him to lay
His wrongs before the chief, and claim from him
That the eſtates the father took by force
The fons ſhould now return: "And weakened
           thus,
'T will then be eafy," cunning Narfi faid,
"To wreak more vengeance on their beggared
           heads;
But 't is deſtruction to oppofe your chief:
Yield to his will; you but delay the hour
Of vengeance; and that hour will furely come."
Then Thorkell, moſt reluctantly, at laſt
Agreed to fend a gentler anſwer back;
And Narfi was defpatched to lay the claims
Before the chief.
              When Olaf heard the caufe
That Narfi brought to him, he fent at once

For Kormak and his brother: heard the whole,
On either fide, and, after much debate,
Decreed a fingle combat fhould decide
The weighty difference that was between them:
Bade them each fend a champion to the lifts;
Appointed time and place; and having learned
From Kormak of his love for Steingerda,
Made the conditions of the battle thefe, —
If Thorkell's champion fhould be overcome,
Thorkell fhould give his daughter to the youth;
But if Kormak fhould fail, the large eftates
That Ogmund took from Thorkell fhould return
Unto their firft poffeffor. The appointed time
Had come; and hence on Battle Ifle were feen
The tents, the buftle, and the armed men;
For here had Olaf fummoned them to meet,
And for the morrow was the combat fet.

While yet alone a few gray lines of light,
And fading ftars, told that the morning hour
Was near at hand, Kormak had left his tent,
And with his brother fought the rocky heights
To catch the early funlight. From his feet,
Far down the precipitous crag, the waves
Came fwelling inward from the open fea,
Dafhing the floating ice upon the fhore,
Grinding to fragments maffes huge as fhips,
And piling mafs on mafs, only to crufh

The whole, as fome great wave came in,
Hurling the weight of many thoufand tons
Light as a bubble on its foaming crefts.
Kormak ftood gazing far away to fea,
Where the dark line of waters met the fky,
On which had now appeared the blufh of dawn,
Faintly reflected in a rofeate tint,
That glimmered on the fea; — but not of dawn,
Nor of the fea, nor of the ocean airs,
That fwept their cooling frefhnefs o'er his brow,
Nor of the combat that a few hours more
Would bring to him, did Kormak think that
      morn.
'Twas no armed brow that rofe above the fea,
And fixed his eye, till faded fea and fky,
And lived alone the vifion, — a fair face,
With curls of golden hair, and deep blue eyes,
In which her gentle heart feemed floating up
To give his own her greeting, met his eye,
And fixed him there enchanted.   A long figh
Swelled in his bofom as the vifion paffed,
Melting again in wave from whence it rofe.
"A woful figh," quoth Thorgils; "I am glad
That 'twas I alone, my lovefick brother,
Who heard that figh; an enemy might fay
You fighed to think of Narfi's ftrength of arm;
But I do think the figh was due to one
Whofe ftrength lies not in arms: no! I am
      wrong;

Two fnowy arms will often move a heart
That hundred-armed Briareus might affail,
And feek to bend in vain.   Liften, brother,
And I will fing a fong will pleafe you now,
Or I will ne'er attempt to fing again.

" I ftood on the rocky ocean-fhore,
    As the waves came wildly rolling in ;
And deep on my ear came the waters' roar,
    And all around me the ocean's din ;

"And my heart fprung out to meet each wave,
    To roll and tofs on its foamy creft ;
For I loved the mufic ocean gave,
    And I longed to plunge on her heaving breaft.

"I lay at night 'mid the pine-trees' fhade,
    And heard them figh as the wind fwept paft;
I loved the fighs that their branches made, —
    The fong they fung with the wind's wild blaft.

"I heard the yelp of the ftraining pack
    When firft to view came the hunted game,
Wildly I echoed the glad founds back,
    And my hunter's heart was all aflame.

"I ftood by the facred Druid-ftone,
    And heard the chant, and the myftic ftrain ;
And I felt a might, beyond my own
    Sweep o'er my foul with the deep refrain.

"I heard the youth with his blithefome fong,
 And the infant lifp his artlefs lay;
My heart has fwept with the ftrains along,
 And bowed itfelf to their fimple fway.

"Laft night we wandered from all apart,
 And, down on the ocean's marge of fand,
I afked the gift of her maiden heart,
 And clafped in my own her trembling hand.

"The deareft found that was ever heard
 Was the whifpered word fhe fpoke to me;
And my own rough heart was as madly ftirred
 By that foft word as man's heart could be.

"O, tell me not of the fongs they fing
 In Odin's palace, above the fkies!
Valhalla! thy halls may wildly ring!
 The fong of the fpheres may round me rife!

"It never can drown that low, fweet tone
 She fpoke laft night on the fandy fhore:
That tone will live in my heart alone,
 When Odin's palace fhall be no more."

As Thorgils ceafed his fong, he turned his eyes
Toward the fpot where Kormak late had been:
The place was vacant; but on looking round,
He faw his brother ftanding on the verge

Of a high cliff that overhung the fea,
Where a ravine cleft the great wall in twain,
And formed a narrow channel, into which
The green waves plunged, but quick were dafhed
    to foam,
And rofe, as white as milk, along the walls,
And then fell back again to join the fwell
Of the next wave advancing ; — there he ftood,
A ftone's-throw off, his plumed cap in his hand;
And on the other fide of the huge rift
Thorgils beheld the fluttering of a drefs,
And, drawing nearer, recognized the face
And the light form of her who fet them free
From Thorkell's power.   They may not need
    me there,
The young man thought, and climbed again the
    rocks
Down to the vale below.   But Kormak ftayed
To hear the lady bid him win her hand,
And take the heart he had already won.
"Dear lady ! this would nerve a feeble hand,
Fill up with daring e'en a coward's heart:
I feel within my heart a power fpring up
I never knew before ; — thy love would lift
A peafant to a king !   Doubt not the end :
If thy fair lips put up their prayer for me,
If thy foft heart appeal unto the gods,
They never can deny you ; — and the charm

Of thy dear love will be a coat of mail
To fence me round about; and Narfi's fword,
Though dug from out the ancient fea-king's
   grave,
And charmed by blood-rites at the midnight
   hour,
In Druid-ring, told by the lips infpired
Of the all-facred priefts, will harmlefs fall
On my broad fhield, thy love."

        " I do truft you,
And yet, with woman's weaknefs, ftill I fear,"
Steingerda faid; "though born and bred 'mid
   wars,
I love not war nor battle; ftill I feel
Proud, my brave foldier, of your ftrength and
   fkill,
And I would have you win an added fame
By your brave deeds to-day. Adieu," fhe faid,
" The fun's bright edge is gleaming o'er the fea:
'T was a ftrange chance by which we met this
   morn ;
But many feet will foon be climbing here,
And curious eyes may mark us."

        " Dearest maid !"
Said Kormak, " I will win the right to-day
To claim your hand, or Battle Ifle fhall be
Wedded to me by death ; this filken fcarf
You gave me once fhall be my talifman,

Your fign of favor, twined around my breaft,
While all is yours within." And fhe was gone —
The waves came dafhing through the narrow way,
And then fwept out again: he marked them not;
A moment ftood, gazing where fhe had been,
Then turned to feek the uneven pathway down;
His mind ftill dreamily away from him,
And ftill her image rofe amid the crags, —
A rugged framing for fo fair a face.

The fun had rifen, but his rays were hid
From the encampment by the rocky wall
That fhut the ocean airs out from the vale,
And caft huge fhadows darkly o'er the pines,
And on the verdant flope. Againft the fky,
So brightly gleaming with the crimfon light
And golden radiance of the morning fun,
The wild and craggy battlemented rocks
Stood black and frowning, till the rifing fun
At length looked o'er their tops, and brightly
        flung
Long golden lines upon the higheft pines;
Danced o'er the groves of birch, juft touched
        with light
The higheft hillocks, calling into life
From every dew-drop richly tinted gems,
That far outfhone the cryftals that they mocked
In their mad blaze of funlight. Now awoke

To active life the ifland vifitors ;
From the white tents poured forth the bufy
     forms ;
From tent to tent run breathlefs meffengers ;
Around the ftandard of their chief were met
The men of note, and Olaf, in their midft,
Received their counfels, as each plan was weighed
And all the laws difcuffed by which they ufed
In thofe old times to fettle every cafe
Wherein a doubt of right and juftice lay.

    The flag of Olaf was an azure field.
Bearing on its centre an ice ifland
Floating upon the fea ; beneath this flag
The chieftain ftood, amid a brilliant throng,
His Thingfmen, powerful chiefs, who only payed
A flight allegiance to their ifland lord,
Acknowledging his power, but fuffered each
To be the fupreme ruler over all
Who dwelt upon his lands ; though once a year
Olaf convened a council of them all,
In which they framed fome neceffary laws,
And made decifion, when the law of arms
Was not appealed to, of each feveral caufe
Of difference that arofe, by any chance,
Within the province. Higher up the mound
O'er which the banner flew had affembled
Many groups of ladies, for now drew near

The appointed hour of battle; and below,
An arrow's flight beyond the chieftain's flag,
Gathered retainers, foldiers, ferfs, and all
Whofe lower rank would not entitle them
To gain a place above; and here a rope,
Faftened to ftakes around a half-circle,
Kept the fpace clear within, — an ample field,
In which the combatants were now to meet,
To meafure ftrength and fkill, and life 'gainft life.

The trumpets founded forth their martial
    notes;
The people fhouted; every eye was turned
Toward the centre. From the throng of chiefs
That ftood round Olaf, Kormak now advanced,
And, kneeling, fwore to abide the judgment,
As battle fhould decide; then took his place
Upon the field, and by his fide, Thorgils,
His fhield-bearer. And Thorkell then ftood
    forth,
Raifed up his aged hands, and took the oath:
Named Narfi as his champion, who at once,
In front of Kormak, took the place affigned
To him; and Thorkell's fon, young Loptur,
    came
To be his fhield-bearer. As they ftood there,
And while the Holmgang laws were read aloud,
All eyes were bent on them; and all was hufhed

Into deep filence, as the herald read.
Each combatant was clad in mail, and held
Upright before him his two-handed fword:
He had no other arms; helmets of fteel,
But viforlefs, — on Kormak's a white plume,
While Narfi's plume was red; iron gantlets
They wore, and over his clofe mail was drawn,
On Kormak's breaft, a filken fcarf of green.
When Narfi firft beheld this fcarf, his eyes
Kindled with rage; for he recognized it
As one his miftrefs had been ufed to wear;
And half he muttered, "That fair filk fhall bear
A deeper ftain, if envy, jealoufy,
And a deep hatred lend me any ftrength."
The fhield-bearers held, each on his right arm
An oval fhield, covered with knobs of brafs;
They wore no mail, nor carried any arm,
Were lightly dreffed; Thorgils had bound his
        brow
With a gold band, wearing nor cap nor plume,
But Loptur's cap was gayly plumed with red.

Again the trumpet notes rung out, — a fign
The combat was begun: lightly they fwung
The heavy fwords above their heads, and moved
Toward each other; eye fixed upon eye,
And every nerve braced up. Kormak ftruck firft,
And Loptur caught the blow upon his fhield,

But reeled and fell beneath the heavy ftroke;
And Narfi's fword cut Thorgils' fhield in two
With its keen edge; then came quick ringing
    blows
As their fwords met; but the trumpets founded,
And called them back. Thorgils' fhield replaced,
    again
They came together; feints and ftratagems,
And heavy blows, and quickly changing place,
Followed each other; their long fwords would
    gleam
Swift through the air; and when you thought the
    blow
Almoft upon the creft, a fhield would flafh
Between. Advancing, Kormak ftumbled, fell,
And Narfi's fword came ftraight above his head,
But Thorgils' fhield caught the defcending blow;
Again his fhield was cleft; and from the helm
Of Kormak, rifing, glanced afide the fword;
Again they clofed, and fword was dafhed on
    fword, —
One blow cut Narfi's fcarlet plume away,
The next glanced downward from his polifhed
    helm,
And broke the mail on his left arm, ftaining
With blood the armor and the fword. Again
The trumpets warned them back; Narfi bound up
IIis wounded arm with Loptur's fcarf, and when

The trumpets founded, rushed upon Kormak
More madly than before, fearing his strength
Would soon be sapped by the fast flowing blood
That moistened all his arm; and Thorgils' shield
Was for the third time cleft; Narfi pressed on,
Struck Kormak on the crest, but his sword broke
With the strong blow, and Kormak, reeling
          back,
At the same moment struck at Narfi's helm,
And dashed him to the earth — they raised him
          up,
But he was stunned, and lay a helpless weight
In Loptur's arms.   A moment, all was still;
Then Kormak, as, bewildered still, he leaned
On his two-handed sword, his father's gift,
Heard a long shout, and then the herald's voice
Proclaiming something, — what, he knew not
          then,
For that last blow, refounding on his helm,
Drowned every sound beside; and now he stood
Beneath the standard.   Olaf grasped his hand,
And he awaked from his bewilderment
To hear the greeting of his friends around,
To catch one glance of fair Steingerda's eye,
As from the throng she passed; yet that one
          glance
Was dearer to him than the thousand words
Of others' praises, — than his triumph even.

Kormak.

CANTO V.

THE SORCERESS.

CANTO V.

THE SORCERESS.

KORMAK and Thorgils, with a gallant band
Of friends, arrived at Tunga, to demand
The forfeit loſt and won at Battle Iſle, —
The hand of fair Steingerda. And Thorkell —
Though rage and paſſion warred within his
  breaſt, —
Though a hot fire blazed fiercely in his heart,
And in each vein the ſcanty blood of age
Thickened and tingled with a youthful force,
Born of his angry paſſion — received them
Moſt graciouſly; and taking Kormak's hand,
Thus anſwered him : —
    "Your father did me wrong,
And I have ſworn revenge ; but that fierce
  oath
The gods who ſway this lower realm of man,

And break and mar each plan that he may make,
To fuit their higher purpofe, have cancelled.
To their power I fain muft yield: 't were
     madnefs
For me, a man, to combat with the gods.
I fwore by Odin's facred ruling arm,
That his arbitrament, by battle fhown,
Should govern me. He has ruled againft me:
My daughter's hand is yours, — one condition
Alone I afk of you. At Spakonfell
Lives one who has a power myfterious
And wonderful over all the fortunes
Of our houfe, — the famous witch Thorveiga.
Perhaps it is the whim of an old man,
To whofe weak age a fecond childhood comes, —
I would afk her favorable affent
Unto this marriage; thus would be removed
A fhapelefs dread that lives within my heart
Of fome impending ill about to fall
Upon the union of your father's fon
With thofe who were your father's bitter foes.
To-night I feaft you as my future fon, —
You and your friends; the hofpitality
Of my poor houfe is yours; to-morrow morn
Seek you alone the witch's mountain hut,
And gain her favor; bring an oracle
Propitious from the gods, breathed through her
     lips,

And the third day I hail you as my fon;
The marriage rites fhall then be duly faid,
And fhe you feek fhall be your wedded wife.
Grant this, — my fuperftition or my whim,
As you may judge it; — it is all I afk."

Once more in Tunga's ancient banquet-hall
Was revelry and feafting ; and old foes
Pledged cup to cup as flowed the ruddy wine,
And hand met hand that never met before
Save in the grafp of battle ; tales of old
Were told to ears that never heard thofe lips
Speak aught but challenge or a battle-cry ;
The clafh of cups outrung the clafh of fwords,
As each fwore friendfhip to his ancient foe.
And Kormak, to his harp, fung in thofe halls,
That heard him once before, — not now dif-
        guifed
By aged garb, but with his youthful limbs
In filken garments clad, and his dark hair
Thrown carelefs backward from his handfome
        face,
Steingerda's fcarf ftill twined about his breaft ;
And all were filent when his fong begun.

" Came Thorbiorn and all his band
    To Mahfahlida's outer wall,
  And loudly beat, with fword in hand ;
    But no one anfwered to his call.

"'Thou thief, Thorarin!' then he cried,
    'Where are the fteeds you ftole from me?
Give up your fpoil, or worfe betide:
    My vengeance now fhall fall on thee!'

"And Black Thorarin ftood within,
    And laughed to hear the chieftain fret;
He faid, 'You curfed me once before,
    But, braggart! I am living yet.'

"Then fpoke Geirrida to her fon, —
    She, the enchantrefs, famed for fkill
In magic art, — 'Well haft thou won
    The name you merit, Sluggard ftill!

"'O flow Thorarin! 'tis not mine,
    The fluggifh current of your life;
Nor did thy fire bequeath it thee:
    He bore no taunt, he fhunned no ftrife.'

"Thorarin heard her taunt, and cried,
    'No more, my mother, peace! I go
To drive the boafter from our gate:
    Think you I fear to meet my foe?'

"Then backward fwung the heavy gate,
    And Black Thorarin ftood befide
His angry foe, and lightly faid,
    'I come to meet the "worfe betide;"'"

" And by his fide his fervants all,
  With fword and buckler, faced the foe ;
To tumult wild the ftrife arofe :
  Sword clafhed on fword, blow followed blow.

" But Ada, Black Thorarin's wife,
  Looked from a cafement in the wall
Down on the court, and 'mid the ftrife,
  She faw her hufband, ftruggling, fall.

" She ftayed no more, but rufhed below,
  Out 'mid the noify, wild warfare,
And caft herfelf before the fword
  Of Thorbiorn, who flew her there.

" But Black Thorarin was not flain ;
  He fell, yet gained again his feet,
To fee his bride rufh wildly forth,
  On Thorbiorn's fword, her death to meet.

" The world fpun round him as he gazed ;
  A fearful cry burft from his lip ;
On Thorbiorn he madly rufhed,
  And cut him down from helm to hip ;

" Then knelt befide his flaughtered wife,
  And took her head upon his breaft ;
' O, fpeak to me again ! ' he faid,
  ' My darling bride ! my deareft ! beft !

"'Thy lips are warm, though pale each cheek,
    Thy pure, dear heart's-blood ſtains thy ſide ;
Speak but one word, ere it be gone !
    Speak but one word ! my wife ! my bride !

"'Alas ! alas ! ſhe will not ſpeak ;
    Mother, bring here your magic art :
Summon each ſpell, and ſtay the blood
    That ebbs ſo ſwiftly from her heart.

"'Your ſpells are vain ! in vain your power !
    You cannot rule the ſtorm you woke !'
His head ſunk down upon his breaſt ;
    With a deep ſigh, his ſad heart broke.

"He never ſpoke, nor raiſed his head ;
    For Thorbiorn's ſword, when Ada fell,
And ſtained its blade with her pure blood,
    Had ſlain with her's his life as well.

"And Geirrida, who ſaw him die,
    Curſed the dread god that gave her power :
'An idle gift you gave to me,
    That ſerves not in the needful hour !

"'Thus they who truſt thee are betrayed :
    A bauble buys a ſoul ſo fair ;
The bauble pleaſes for an hour ;
    The hour is paſt, — then comes deſpair !'

" That god — dread Loki — heard her curfe,
    And crufhed her in his angry might ;
One frenzied fhriek rung wildly forth,
    As plunged her foul in endlefs night."

The fong was ended, and a wild applaufe
Greeted the youthful bard ; for every heart,
Fraught with the fuperftition of the age,
Felt the ftrange thrill that fuperftition lends
To tales of wild adventure ; every heart,
Though feldom tutored to a gentle thought,
Turned from the din of battle to lament
With Black Thorarin for his flaughtered wife.
And thus the feaft went on ; and midnight came
And paffed, and left them at their revels ftill.

At midnight, to the chamber of their chief
Oddur and Gudmund came ; and Narfi led
Them there, where, while the feaft and fong
       went on
And revelry below, a plan was made.
Oddur and Gudmund took their chief's
       commands,
And, filently as they had come, retired.
Narfi difmiffed them from the weftern gate,
Watching them till the dufk of Night had clofed
Around her children ; then he paffed within,
And muttered, " Now at laft it will be done :

The brothers will not fail; the brutes would
    ftrike
At fleeping Odin, if their fwords were paid
To fhed his blood.   Yes: the fudden onflaught
And their great ftrength muft give them victory,
If they obey directions.   To make fure,
Before 't is daylight I will go myfelf
To fee the work performed ; I have defigned
To afk Thorveiga what the future has
In ftore for me.   I have, in truth, no faith
That fhe can tell me more than I could tell
Of what muft come with time ; but I would fee
Her whom the people fear ; would try my heart.
I never feared a mortal being yet,
So, dread Thorveiga, drop your Gorgon fhield,
For fuperftition has no power o'er me."

Up, amid rocks and crags, at Spakonfell
Thorveiga dwelt, a forcerefs renowned
Through all the ifland ; a rude ftone-built hut,
Raifed 'gainft a caverned cleft in the huge rock
That frowned precipitous above, was her home.
Here, with her fons, fhe lived, apart from all,
In this wild, defolate, and lone ravine.
Her name was fpoken with a trembling dread,
And none had feen her fave the daring few
Who fought her hut to learn from her what fates
Lay darkly in the future, or to feek

A talifman wrought by her magic fpells
And myftic power, — invulnerable mail,
A fhield no fword could cleave, a thrice-charmed
     fword,
Obtained by midnight fpell from fome old ghoft,
Conjured to earth again by her dread power, —
A fword now gifted with ftrange ftrength to kill.
None ventured near the rocks where fhe abode,
And feldom was her dreaded name pronounced,
For all remembered Ulfar, and his death.
He was a hunter, who, delayed by night,
Waited until the moon arofe, for light
To find his way down the rough mountain-fide.
On the high rock that overhung the hut
Where dwelt Thorveiga and her brutifh fons
He paufed a moment in his fteep defcent ;
And there he faw ftrange fights. A hundred
     ghofts
Were dancing round a fpectral wizard fire ;
The dread forcerefs, Oddur, and Gudmund
Were mingling gayly with their midnight guefts,
And dancing wildly to a difmal tune,
Beat on phantom drums by fkeleton arms ;
And all the rocky dell was filled with forms
Strange and uncouth. And Ulfar, trembling, faw
The moonbeams fhining through tranfparent
     fhapes
From which no fhadows fell; he faw, and fwooned

7

On the cold rock, nor waked until the fun
With morning beams fhone on his frozen limbs,
And warmed them into life. Then with flow fteps
He left the fpot, but caft one frightened glance
Into the dell below. All now was ftill
And lifelefs, and no fign remained of thofe
That he had feen dancing beneath the moon.
He told his friends, with trembling tongue, the
       tale ;
But from that hour his ftrength ebbed flow away,
And ere the feafon paffed away he died ;
And it was whifpered that he went to join
The ghofts that danced before Thorveiga's hut.

Within her hut the Sorcerefs now fat,
And twirled her flying wheel, from which the yarn
Spun rapidly. No light of day was there :
The hut was windowlefs, and from the cleft
And ragged cavern in the rock beyond
All light was clofe fhut out, fave what was fhed
O'er all around from a huge filver lamp,
Hung from the ceiling by a chain of bronze.
Upon the walls were ftrangely mingled fhield
And fword, with the ftuffed fkins of fnake and
       toad,
Lizard and tortoife ; whitened bones, that feemed
As if of human kind. But fhe who fat,
Her muttering mingling with the noify wheel,

The living inmate of this ſtrange abode,
Herſelf was ſtranger than all elſe around :
A ſtately woman, with a pale, wild face,
O'er which fell ſtraggling locks of raven hair,
Laced here and there with threads of ſilver hue.
A gown of black was robed around her form,
From which contraſted, deathly pale, her face
And her half-naked breaſt. She raiſed her head,
Threw back her hair with thin and trembling
          hands,
And ſtopped her rapid wheel, that ſhe might hear
With more diſtinctneſs the faint ſounds without
That came to her quick ear; for now the ſound
Of footſteps came along the rocky path
Up to the doorway.   " It is a ſtranger,"
Thorveiga muttered, as ſhe raiſed the latch
In anſwer to his knocking.   The daylight
Came flooding inward through the opening door,
Struggling a moment in the darkened hut
With the pale lamplight; and with the daylight
Narfi ſtepped o'er the threſhold. The door cloſed,
And, ere the youth could bear the change of light
Upon his eyes, Thorveiga once more ſat
Beſide her wheel, and plied the buſy thread
Then Narfi doffed his cap to her, and ſaid :
" I come, good mother, by your aid, to look
Beyond the preſent to the time to come.
Love and ambition, tell me of their fate,

And how to guide my fteps in the dark way
Through which I pafs ! "
                        When Narfi firft appeared,
The Sorcerefs had caft a quick, keen glance
On him, ere fhe refumed her feat. That glance
Narfi had loft. When now fhe heard him fpeak,
Her hands fell idly by her fide, her breath
Came gafpingly ; but ftill the wheel fped on,
Nor did fhe raife her eyes. The youth drew forth
A purfe of gold, and dropped it at her feet.
Thorveiga raifed her eyes : "Your name," fhe
        faid,
" Is Narfi ; your father's name you know not ;
Why afk you not that, by my magic art,
I fhould reveal your birth and parentage ? "

The ruby color fled from Narfi's lip :
"If you have power," he faid, "I bid you fpeak ! "

" If I have power ! " the Sorcerefs replied ;
" Liften and judge : you feek from me to know
The end of your ambition and your love ?
You love Steingerda, daughter to Thorkell,
And your ambition is to gain the place
That Thorkell's death will vacate. Yours by
        right
That place fhould be, for *you are Thorkell's fon!*
Well may you ftart ; but liften to me ftill.

" Many years ago, near Tajaldnes dwelt
Leidolf Kappa.   His dwelling was a tower,
Rough-built of ftone, that ftood by the fea-fhore.
The coaft was wild and rocky ; but, beneath
The maffive rocks on which the tower was built,
A narrow beach came up againft the wall,
And every tide fwept fmooth the fnow-white fand
As it rolled out to fea.   One ftormy night,
When the wild waves came plunging up the fands
To dafh upon the rocks, Thorunna fat,
And, from a window in the lofty tower
Gazed o'er the troubled fea ; fhe watched each
    wave,
As, capped with foam, it dafhed refiftlefs on,
And broke to atoms in a tumult wild
Of mingled foam and fpray ; when on the fea,
Red, 'mid the lines of white, fhe faw a light
Come moving in from the wild wafte without,
As though fome barque was fteered toward the
    light
That glimmered from their walls.   Swift it
    came on,
And fcarce the maid could warn her fire and
    friends
To haften to the fpot, when the barque, borne
On the high top of a huge furging wave,
Dafhed on the founding rock.   One man alone
Of all her crew was faved from death that night.

That man was your fire, Thorkell; wounded,
     stunned,
And helpless, he was thrown within the reach
Of Leidolf and his friends, who rescued him
From the fierce wave, that would have drawn
     him back
Into the angry sea.   They took him up,
Conveyed him to the tower, brought back the life
To his dead limbs, to his cold heart again.
And many anxious hours beside his couch
Thorunna sat, and watched him as he slept,
Or as he struggled feebly for his life
In fever's burning grasp.   But youth at last
Gained triumph o'er disease; his strength came
     back,
And still his gentle nurse sat by his side,
And cheered his weary hours. He did her wrong:
Won her young heart, deceived her, and then fled.
You are his son and hers.   Her father died.
Uni, a wild sea-rover, one dark night
Landed his crew upon the sands, and took
From weak Thorunna her lone tower. Thy youth
Was passed upon the deck of his light barque.
When you grew older you rebelled 'gainst him,
Seduced his sailors from allegiance to him,
Slew him at night amid his helpless sleep,
And brought your service here unto Thorkell,
Although you knew not that he was your fire."

While Thorveiga told this ſtrange hiſtory,
Narfi had ſtood with pallid cheeks, his hands
Clenched in his ſtrong emotion. "Is this true?"
He cried; " or have you conjured up the tale
But to deceive me? True, I ſlew Uni.
He ſtruck me on my cheek, called me baſtard;
I waited till the night, and then he died.
Thorkell my ſire! Ambition! now I ſee
The road by which to mount.

Thorveiga ſaid:
" Have you no thought of her who gave you
birth?
Whether alive or dead?"

"Speak on!" he ſaid,
"And tell me all. Mother! the very word
Sounds ſtrangely to my ear; yet in my mind,
Dim, like a dream, comes back a gentle face
That ſmiled upon me once."

"That face was mine!"
The Sorcereſs exclaimed. "Yes, I am ſhe,
Thorunna, who once dwelt in that lone tower
Upon the ſea-ſhore; ſhe whom Thorkell wronged,
Who nurſed thy youth till madneſs drove her
forth;
She who by madneſs gained the myſtic gift
Of prophecy. I have watched over you,
Known of each chance that time has ever brought,
But found, alas! that I was powerleſs

To aid you,—fome ftronger force controlled you.
Nor can I read *your* future.   All is hid
From me beyond the prefent of your fate."
She held her thin, white hands outftretched to
    him,
And Narfi trembled when thofe hands touched
    his.

  " Mother," he faid, " thy gift of prophecy
Defcends to me.   Thorkell has lived too long ;
'T is time we were avenged — "
                    " 'T is not by thee,
My fon, fhall Thorkell die.   I know his fate ;
The ftars have told me how his end fhall be.
The time approaches, but 't is not *thy* hand
Muft cut his thread of life." But while fhe fpoke
The found of ftruggling feet, the clafh of fwords,
Was heard without the hut.   Narfi ftarted,
And raifed the latch.   Thorveiga called aloud :
" Stay, ftay, my fon ; the future comes to me,
And dangers clufter now around your head ! "
But he ftayed not, —fprung through the open-
    ing door,
And left her.   For a moment fhe ftood ftill,
With eyes bent down, as though upon the earth
She read, in her own myftic charaƈters,
What time now wrote in the material type
Of aƈt and deed without.   Then to the door,

With a wild and pitiful cry, fhe fprung,
And ftaggered o'er the threfhold, — the firft time
In twenty years the funlight fell on her.

  Kormak and Thorgils with the dawn fet forth
To pay the promifed vifit to the hut
Of the witch Thorveiga. The hills were paffed;
They clambered up the deep ravine, and now
Drew near her defolate and lone abode,
When Thorgils, who went firft, felt a fharp wound
Piercing his fide, and heard the bowftring's
          twang, —
Saw two huge figures leap adown the rock
Before him : drew his fword, and flew Oddur
With his firft blow.   But now the heavens
          whirled round,
And in a dream he fell.   With a wild cry
Kormak rufhed on, as the giant Gudmund
Raifed his right arm to flay the proftrate youth,
And dafhed his fword afide.   Now, o'er the form
Of Thorgils their fwords met and rung again
In defperate battle.   As Gudmund fell
Never to rife, down from Thorveiga's hut,
With defperate purpofe gleaming in his eyes,
His face ftill pale, rufhed Narfi, with fword
          drawn,
And took the giant's place. "Now you or I,"
He faid, " fight our laft fight ! "

             " Not all the lives
Of all the houſe of Thorkell will repay
My brother's death!" Kormak replied to him.
"You ſhall go firſt; the reſt ſhall follow you,
If that dear life be ſlain. You ſhall go firſt!
I feel the ſtrength of all my warrior ſires
Come to me now. Back, back to death you go!"
And Narfi's blood was flowing faſt; forced back,
He fell upon his knee, beheld the ſword
Of Kormak blazing in the air above,
Then ſaw no more of earth. Forth from her hut,
Her hair diſhevelled and her eyes on fire,
Thorveiga came, and raiſed her fallen ſon,
Tore off her robes to ſtanch his flowing blood,
But came too late to ſave; his head fell back
Upon her arm, and Narfi's ſoul had fled.
The Sorcereſs aroſe, ſtretched her thin hand
Toward the ſky, and called upon the gods
To ſmite his ſlayer. "Wherefore ſtrike ye not?
Odin, great Thor, Thorveiga calls on ye!
They heed me not. Then let him live!" ſhe cried;
" My curſe ſhall follow him: his life be ſhort,
But filled with pains and anguiſh; diſappoint
His deareſt hopes; cruſh every joy of life,
And make his path as deſolate and drear
As mine hath been; let his death be cruel,
Bloody, terrible. By every ſpell
Of magic art I call deſtrućtion down

On his doomed head ! And in his lateſt hour
May I be there to curſe his paſſing ſoul,
As from the earth it flies ! ”
                       But Kormak kneeled
Beſide his brother, drew the arrow forth,
And ſtanched his blood ; called back the life again
To his white lips and to his half-cloſed eyes,
Nor heard, nor heeded then, her fearful curſe.

Kormak.

CANTO VI.

THE MARRIAGE.

CANTO VI.

THE MARRIAGE.

WHILE by his brother's fick-couch Kor-
     mak fat,
And tended him gently as a fifter,
Forgetting other love, and e'en revenge,
Remembering only that deep, ftrong love
That bound him to his brother; while his hand
Held to his fevered lips the cooling draught,
And fmoothed his weary pillow, as he bent
O'er him while fleeping, held in his the hand
That burned with pain and fever, — at Tunga,
Thorkell was brooding over what had chanced,
And dwelling on the future; and alone
He fat, gloomy, within the deepening gloom
Of his own chamber, when Steingerda came
And knelt befide his knee, and took his hand,
In filence watched his clofe-contracted brow
And firm-fet lips. At laft fhe fpoke to him: —

"Father," she said, "give up your fiercer
    thought,
I pray of you; the anger that you nurse
Gnaws, like a vulture, deeply in your heart,
Writes suffering on your brow, helps the years
To bow your frame, works more than even time
On you. Forgive the wrong you bore of old;
Forgive his son of old who injured you.
'T is noble to forgive, — a braver part
Than, by opposing gods and men, to bring
Destruction on us all. Father, I love
Him whom you seek to kill, — destroying him,
You strike my heart as well: his heart is mine,
As mine is his, — my life with his is joined.
I pray you soften down your ancient hate,
Pardon the past, remember not old wrongs!"

While thus she pleaded, Thorkell's firm-set face
Relaxed not line nor muscle, and his eye
Turned on her face its unrelenting glance.
"Thou art no daughter of my blood," he said,
"If thou dost love my hated enemy,
The son of him who wronged both me and mine,
Thee, being mine, and all our kindred house,
And now himself hath slain my servants true,
And braved my anger with an idle boast,
And armed my prince in wrath against our house:
Is this the way to quench the old-time feud?

A fitting marriage this would be indeed !
Blood lies between you, a red, warning ftream,
And you would dip your garments in the ftain,
Would hold the hand whofe kindred fhed my
    blood,
Would fwear to love where you fhould give
    but hate !
Shame on you, daughter ! you are none of mine ;
Your mother muft have wronged me. Say no
    more !
When you can ftay the waves that wafh our fhores,
And heap their maffes up againft the fky ;
When you can change the froft to fummer's heat,
Melt the vaft iceberg with befeeching eye ;
When you can call the fun down from above,
Blot out the moon, and dim the fhining ftars, —
Then may you hope to move me. Tears are vain ;
Their feeble drops hifs on my burning heart,
And feed its blazing fires. Away ! away,
Before I curfe the child that loves my foes
Better than me or mine ! " He fhook her off,
And, trembling both with rage and paffion, ftood
A fearful image of unbridled rage.
Then with quick footfteps, nervous and infirm,
He paced the room.
               And Steingerda replied :
" Curfe me not, father ; do not curfe the child
Who loves thee now and ever. None the lefs

8

My love for thee, — who gave my life its life,
To whom my heart now clings as firm as clings
The ivy to the ſtrong, ſuſtaining oak,
Neſtling round its great trunk, — becauſe, alas!
Another love than thine muſt ſhare with thine.
I *gave* not love, but loved unwillingly,
Knowing thou call'ſt him foe: could not but love,
Deſpite myſelf and thee, and every thought
That bade my heart beat coldly; and my heart
Grew with my love, nor gave thee ſmaller place
Becauſe his place was there.   Forgive, forget,
And curſe me not becauſe my heart ſpeaks out,
Confiding all to thee."
                              When the ſunſhine
Falls on the high ice-plain, cold and frigid
It caſts the bright reflection off, — melts not,
Yields not; as ſtony-hearted as that plain,
As coldly unrelenting, Thorkell heard,
But gave no word of anſwer, ſave to bid
Her leave him; and ſadly ſhe obeyed him.

   Alone again with thought, he nurſed revenge,
Repeating to himſelf: " I will not change,
And baſely give my hand where I have ſworn
To give the ſword's edge; not though Odin ſend,
In his great thunder tones, divine commands,
And light his meſſenger with all the glare
Of the keen lightning! His power may cruſh me,

But it can never change : my foul at leaft
Is all my own, nor gods nor men shall bend
Its earneft purpofe ! "
                        'Mid his reverie
Came one to fpeak with him ; and there entered
A woman, dreffed in black, with a mafked face
And ftately air.   The thin, pale hand, half hid
Amid the folds of her dark robe, was that
Which held the head of Narfi when the life
Flowed from his breaft with the dark crimfon
            ftream
That Kormak's fword had freed.   Long they
            fat there
In confultation, and when they parted
Thorkell faid : "Thou wilt not fail ! Remember
His, the Venetian cup, and he muft drink
Oblivion to the paft."
                        She anfwered :
" He fhall drink oblivion, and the wrongs
That time has gathered, unavenged, fhall then
Find retribution.   Doubt it not ; bring thou
The nuptials fpeedily, — I will not fail."

For the third time we vifit Tunga's halls
Amid feftivity ; for on this night
The daughter of the houfe fhall wed its foe,
And bridge by her alliance the deep gulf
That long has yawned between. When Steingerda

Heard Thorkell bid to deck herfelf in robes
Meet for her wedding with the man fhe loved,
While yet his bitter and paffionate words
Of enmity were ringing in her ears,
She feared that rage had overpreffed his brain,
And made him mad.

      " My father, late you faid
I muft not love him, for he was thy foe ;
And now you bid me wed him ! you are changed ?

  Thorkell replied : " I looked behind the veil,
And found thy marriage was a thing decreed.
I may not war with fate, for deftiny
Laughs at man's feeble efforts, and fweeps on
Its full, ftrong tide, regardlefs of us all.
To-night you wed ; to-night fhall Kormak ceafe
To bear my hate ; too long, by far too long,
Has he been hated."

      While fhe heard his words,
She looked in vain for kindnefs in his eye
To match the gentler fpeech, and to her heart
There came a fad diftruft, a boding fenfe
Of fome calamity.   More in forrow
Than in joy fhe clad herfelf in gay robes,
And waited for her bridegroom ; and at eve
He came, and Thorgils, with a cheek ftill pale,
But with recovery beaming in his eye,
And many friends were with him.   As fhe faw

Her lover, felt the thrill when their hands met,
Read his love in every paffionate glance
That paffed between them, her fad foreboding
Vanifhed as night at funrife, and dear thoughts,
Fair anticipations for the future,
Came to her heart, and banifhed every fear.

And Thorkell gave them welcome in few words;
His mind feemed abfent, brooding on fome
        thought;
And oft he ftarted, and looked wildly round,
Then funk again in moodinefs; but when,
Each in his place in the great banquet-hall,
The hour had come to pledge his ancient foe
And call him fon, the old man roufed himfelf,
And bade the wine be poured; each cup was
        filled
With dancing, fparkling drops. "My fon," he
        faid,
And raifed his cup, "the wrongs are now atoned
That long have warred between thy houfe and
        mine, —
I drink with thee — *Oblivion to the paft.*"

And Kormak gazed on the fair face of her
Whom now he wedded, raifed the cryftal bowl,
And drank the fparkling wine; each cup was
        drained.

While empty goblets clattered on the board,
Rofe the long fhout of "Kormak and his bride!"
"Live, Kormak and his bride!" Thorkell fpoke
      not,
But gazed, like one entranced, on him who now
Claimed kindred with his houfe.
              As the cry ceafed,
A dark-robed form, that ftood within a niche
Concealed by drooping foldings of a flag
That fwept from ceiling to the oaken floor, —
The tattered banner of an old fea-king, —
Came wildly through their midft, threw back
      her hood,
And bared her pallid face, o'er which there fell,
In tangled maffes and in elfin locks,
Her long gray hair; and every breath was hufhed,
And every heart beat flower, as fhe poured
A cup of wine, and raifed it to her lips.

    " Thorveiga drinks your pledge," fhe cried
      aloud ;
" Thorkell, remembereft thou the wronged maid
Of the lone tower upon the ocean cliff ?
Thorunna comes again to drink with thee
Thy lateft pledge, ' Oblivion to the paft.'
Kormak, I drink to thee ; my fon you flew,
But here I pledge ' Oblivion to the paft.'
Why ftand ye awed ?   I drink to all of ye.

What! feel ye yet the poifon in your veins?
Works the drugged wine on ye fo foon, fo foon?"

And every face grew pale, the blood froze chill
In each cold heart, as, with her arms upraifed
And burning eyes, the Sorcerefs fpoke on :
"Thorkell, you bade me poifon but one cup:
Lo, I have poifoned all ! Ye all have drunk,
And I with you, the fatal pledge of death !
Now pales the blood in warrior cheeks, and now
Chills round your boaftful hearts the ice of death !
Your keen-edged fwords, your fhining fuits of
         mail,
Avail not now, — the foe has paffed within.
No power can fave ye ; with a gallant train
Thorveiga marches to the world beyond,
And wronged Thorunna takes at laft revenge."

Thorkell had ftarted when Thorunna's name
Firft paffed her lips; for with that name there
         rufhed
A flood of recollection back to him,
And in her fearful, pallid face he traced
The wreck of beauty that was hers of old ;
Her fair young face came back before his eye,
The while its ghoftly, dread reality
Mocked at his recollection, with the change
That years and wrongs had written on her brow;

And the old wrong rofe up before his mind,
And, while the poifon thickened in his veins
And froze his heart, his confcience froze his foul.

The deadly poifon mingled with the wine
Preyed inftant on each life. Scarce time had they
To bid a laft farewell to friends around,
Ere the fell ficknefs crufhed the germ of life,
And Death transfixed them with his fatal fpear.
One kifs, one laft embrace, and, hand in hand,
The wedded lovers fought their bridal bed
In the cold halls of death; and Thorgils kneeled,
Kiffing his brother's lips, and kiffing died;
And many fled from out the fatal hall,
But in their flight they died.   Not one of thofe
Who drank that pledge, but drank the draught
        of death.

And years rolled on : in Tunga's ancient hall
There dwelt no inmate; for the walls were curfed,
And gliding ghofts were feen at midnight hour;
And, as the wind a moment hufhed its fweep
Round thofe dread walls, within the goblins
        fhrieked,
And drank again — " Oblivion to the paft ! "

THE END.